This book belongs to

Bluebell Glade

Dandelion Dell

Heart of Misty Wo[od]

Hawthorn Hedgerows

ather Hill

Sundown Hill

ystal Cave

Golden Meadow

Moonshine Pond

Dewdrop Spring

neydew Meadow

rry Bushes

Misty Wood Rabbit Warren

HOME
SWEET
HOME

How many Fairy Animals books have you collected?

- ✓ Chloe the Kitten
- Bella the Bunny
- Paddy the Puppy
- Mia the Mouse

And there are more magical adventures coming very soon!

Fairy Animals
of Misty Wood

Chloe the Kitten

Lily Small

Henry Holt and Company
New York

With special thanks to Thea Bennett

Henry Holt and Company
Publishers since 1866
175 Fifth Avenue
New York, NY 10010
mackids.com

Henry Holt® is a registered trademark of Macmillan
Publishing Group, LLC.
Text copyright © 2013 by Hothouse Fiction Ltd.
Illustrations copyright © 2013 by Kirsteen Harris-Jones
Cover illustration copyright © John Francis
All rights reserved.

First published in the United States in 2015 by
Henry Holt and Company
Originally published in Great Britain in 2013 by
Egmont UK Limited.

Library of Congress Cataloging-in-Publication Data
Small, Lily.
Chloe the kitten / Lily Small. — First American edition.
pages cm. — (Fairy animals of Misty Wood ; [1])
"First published in the United States in 2015 by Henry Holt and Company, LLC."
Summary: Chloe, a Cobweb Kitten, is fluttering through Hawthorn Hedgerows
in the enchanted realm of Misty Wood, decorating cobwebs with dewdrops
when she meets a baby mouse who is lost and afraid.
ISBN 978-1-62779-141-0 (pbk.) — ISBN 978-1-62779-360-5 (e-book)
[1. Fairies—Fiction. 2. Cats—Fiction. 3. Mice—Fiction.
4. Lost children—Fiction.]
I. Title.
PZ7.S635Chl 2015   [Fic]—dc23   2014026456

Henry Holt books may be purchased for business or promotional use. For information on
bulk purchases, please contact Macmillan Corporate and Premium Sales Department at
(800) 221-7945 x5442 or by e-mail at specialmarkets@macmillan.com.

First American Edition—2015
Printed in the United States of America by LSC Communications,
Harrisonburg, Virginia

10

 # Contents

CHAPTER ONE

Good Morning, Misty Wood

It was early morning in Misty Wood. The moon had long since snuggled into his starry bed, and the sun was just beginning to stretch into the sky.

In a cozy cot made of moss and grass, in a tiny home tucked under the roots of an old chestnut tree, a kitten named Chloe was waking up. She yawned and rubbed the end of her button nose with a velvety paw. Then she opened her eyes and looked at her dandelion clock.

"Oh no! I'm late!" she cried, leaping from her bed. But she stopped short when she caught

sight of herself in the small pool of
water she used as a mirror.

"Puppy tails and poppy seeds!"
she meowed. "I can't go out like
this!"

Chloe's whiskers were flat because she had slept on them. Quickly, she licked her paws and stroked her whiskers until they were shiny and smooth. Then she twisted her head and looked down to check her glittery fairy wings.

You see, Chloe was no ordinary kitten. She was a Cobweb Kitten, one of the many fairy animals who lived in Misty Wood. Every fairy animal in Misty Wood had

a special job to do to make sure it stayed such a beautiful place.

The Bud Bunnies used their twitchy noses to ease flowers into bloom.

The Hedgerow Hedgehogs used their spikes to pick up leaves and keep the ground tidy.

The Holly Hamsters nibbled the holly leaves into shape for Christmas.

And the Cobweb Kittens

5

decorated the cobwebs in the trees with glistening dewdrops so that they sparkled and shone.

Chloe patted her wings into place and smiled down at her reflection.

"Perfect," she purred. "Now I'm ready for work." She picked up her special dewdrop-collecting basket, which had been woven from flower stems.

"No time for breakfast today,"

she said, looking longingly at the acorn cup of milk on her conker table.

The magical spring where the Cobweb Kittens got their dewdrops came to life only while the sun was rising. She had to get there quickly or she would miss it.

Chloe padded over to the door and flung it open. Outside, it was as if Misty Wood was just stirring itself from sleep. A breeze whispered

7

through the trees, making all the branches sway.

Chloe could hear the first chirps of the birds as they got ready to sing. She opened her wings. They shimmered purple and pink in the first morning light.

"Good morning, Misty Wood!" she said, fluttering up into the air.

Chloe swooped through the trees and out into Bluebell Glade. Down below her she could hear the

tinkle of hundreds of flowery bells as they bobbed in the breeze. She breathed in the bluebells' sweet scent and continued on her way. As she left the glade, she came to Heather Hill.

It matches my wings, Chloe thought with a smile as she looked down at the carpet of purple heather.

Next, she did a loop-the-loop over Golden Meadow, hoping to

10

catch sight of the playful Pollen Puppies flicking the golden flower pollen with their tails. But the cheeky pups were asleep, curled up on their cushions of moss.

Chloe floated on, enjoying the sleepy silence. The meadow below her looked like a rainbow painted across the land. There were flowers of every color.

Then she came to Moonshine Pond. The Moonbeam Moles had

been working hard all night, flying through the sky and dropping moonbeams into the pond to make it look pretty. Now the water had a beautiful pearly glow. It reminded Chloe of the cup of milk in her kitchen, and she suddenly felt very thirsty. She looked at the brightening sky. The sun wasn't quite up yet. As long as she was quick, she should have enough time for a drink.

Chloe flew down and landed on the soft bank of the pond. Putting her basket next to her, she leaned forward to lap the sweet water with her tiny pink tongue. She was careful to be quiet. She didn't want to wake the little moles, who had just gone to bed.

Mmm, Chloe thought. *That's better!* The water was delicious. The moonbeams made it taste as sweet as honey. Chloe licked her lips,

13

unfurled her wings, and fluttered

off again.

At last she came to a beautiful

valley. In the middle of the valley

14

lay a shimmering lake. Silvery mist drifted across the surface of the water. Suddenly, as the first rays of sunlight peeped over the treetops and touched the lake, a jet of water rose high into the air, like a fountain. Fat, glistening dewdrops fell like sparkles from a fairy's wand.

Chloe breathed a sigh of relief. She had arrived at Dewdrop Spring just in time.

The air was filled with excited

meowing and purring. There were Cobweb Kittens everywhere! Fluttering their wings as fast as they could, they headed toward the spring, scooping up dewdrops in their special collecting baskets. Every kitten needed to work very hard if all the cobwebs in Misty Wood were to be covered in dewdrops.

"Hello, Chloe," a little tabby kitten called as he flew past.

"Hurry up! You're late!" a white kitten cried, her fairy wings glistening silver and gold.

"Here I come!" Chloe called happily to her friends. "Save some for me!" With a flick of her wings, she dived toward the fountain, ready to collect the dewdrops with her basket. But as she held out her paws, she noticed something terrible.

Her basket was missing!

17

CHAPTER TWO

A Helpful Friend

Chloe gave a sad little meow. What could have happened to her basket? Then she remembered. She had set it down on the bank of

Moonshine
Pond when she
stopped for a
drink. She must

have forgotten to pick it up.

"Whiskers and whirlpools!
Whatever am I going to do?" Chloe
cried. She looked anxiously at
the sky.

It was getting lighter and
lighter! There was no time for her to
go all the way back to Moonshine

Pond. Soon the sun would be up, and Dewdrop Spring would disappear for another day. Then there would be no dewdrops for her to collect, and she wouldn't be able to decorate her cobwebs.

She watched as, one by one, the other Cobweb Kittens filled their baskets and flew away. Her cobwebs would be the only empty ones in all of Misty Wood!

Chloe flopped down on a patch

of grass and put her fluffy head in her paws. A tear trickled slowly down her nose.

"If I can't decorate my cobwebs, I'll be the worst Cobweb Kitten ever," she sobbed.

"And why can't you decorate your cobwebs?" a cheery voice asked from behind her.

Chloe turned and peeked out from between her paws. A Stardust Squirrel was sitting on a log in

23

front of her, holding an acorn.

Chloe sighed. Normally, she would be pleased to see a Stardust Squirrel.

Stardust Squirrels were some of the most beautiful creatures in Misty Wood. Their soft fur was a glittery gray color, and their wings were a delicate silver and white. When they shook their bushy tails, they sent a shimmer of stardust floating over all the leaves in the

wood, making them glimmer and sparkle.

"I left my basket at Moonshine Pond," Chloe whispered. "Now I can't collect any dewdrops."

"And why did you leave your basket at Moonshine Pond?" the squirrel asked with a twirl of his whiskers.

"Because I'd put it down so I could have a drink," Chloe said, feeling very ashamed.

"I see," said the squirrel. "And why did you need a drink?"

"Because I didn't have any breakfast."

"Oh, you must never leave the house without having breakfast," the squirrel said with a twinkle in his eye. He hopped off the log and bounded over to Chloe, leaving a glittery trail behind him. "I always have a bowl of acorns for breakfast. I was just collecting

26

some, actually." The squirrel held out his acorn to her. "Here, do you want one?"

Chloe shook her head.

The squirrel looked thoughtful for a moment. "What you really need is a walnut," he said.

"No, thank you. I'm much too sad to be hungry," Chloe replied.

The Stardust Squirrel gave a gentle laugh. It sounded like the tinkle of ice crystals on a frozen

lake. "I don't mean to eat," he said. "I mean to make a basket."

Chloe frowned. How could she use a walnut as a basket?

"Wait here," the squirrel said.

Chloe watched as he scampered over to a small tree stump on the bank of the lake, scattering a trail of stardust as he ran. "Ta-da!" he cried, rummaging around in the tree stump. "Just the thing!" He pulled out half a walnut shell.

Chloe looked at the wrinkled shell. "That doesn't look much like a basket," she said sadly.

"Not yet," the squirrel agreed. "But just you watch."

Quick as a flash, the squirrel nibbled two little holes into the side of the shell. Then he picked a thick blade of grass, and with a blur of paws and a flurry of stardust, he tied the grass to the walnut shell to make a sturdy handle.

"Oh, I see!" Chloe exclaimed.
"It's a perfect dewdrop-collecting
basket. Thank you!"

"You're welcome," said the squirrel. "Now, are you sure you don't want this tasty acorn?"

Chloe smiled and shook her head. "No, thank you. I've got work to do. Good-bye!" And with that, she flew up into the air and over to the spring.

Flapping her wings hard, Chloe swooped this way and that, catching glistening dewdrops as she flew. The walnut shell was

32

bigger than her old basket, so she was able to collect more drops than ever before.

Just as Chloe had filled her basket, the sun finished rising above the trees. At once, Dewdrop Spring sank back into the lake.

"Just in time," Chloe said to herself as she fluttered through the valley and off to Hawthorn Hedgerows, the part of Misty Wood she was in charge of decorating.

Hawthorn Hedgerows was right by the edge of the wood. As Chloe flew closer, she spotted the silvery strings of a delicate cobweb clinging to the first hedge. She shivered with excitement. She would soon make it look beautiful.

"I have just the dewdrops for you," Chloe said with a smile as she hovered close to the web. She chose the smallest and sparkliest dewdrops from her basket and

carefully hung them one by one on the threads.

After she had filled the cobweb with dewdrops, she flew back a bit to check her work. The cobweb now sparkled like a jewel! Eagerly, Chloe flew over to the next web and began again. As she worked, she hummed a little tune. She felt so glad to be able to decorate her cobwebs after all.

Chloe was starting her fifth

cobweb when she felt a gentle

tap on the top of her head. She

looked up and saw a spider

dangling above her on a strand of
silky web.

"Sorry to trouble you," the
spider said, pointing a spindly
leg toward the part of the hedge
Chloe had just finished. "But I
was wondering why you haven't
decorated my web."

"I have!" Chloe answered in
surprise. "Look, I'll show you." She
spread her wings and flew back
along the hedge. But to her dismay,

she saw that the spider was right.
His cobweb was empty! There
were no dewdrops on it at all.
And all the other cobwebs Chloe
had spent so long decorating
were bare, too. Her dewdrops had
completely disappeared!

CHAPTER THREE

The Dewdrop Thief

Chloe flew this way and that, searching for the dewdrops. They were nowhere to be seen.

"I told you," the spider said,

while solemnly blinking his tiny eyes.

"But I just don't understand!" Chloe meowed. "I'm sure I did that hedgerow. Look, it was the same as this one."

Chloe turned to show the spider the hedge she had just begun to decorate with sparkly dewdrops. But much to her surprise, they were gone, too!

"Someone must have stolen

them!" Chloe cried. She gulped. *Someone . . . or something.*

"You mean we have a dewdrop thief?" the spider asked, frowning.

Chloe nodded. "I'm afraid so."

"I don't like the sound of that," said the spider, and he scurried off as fast as his eight legs would carry him.

Chloe slumped down to the ground. "Whatever will I tell the other fairy animals?" she sighed. "They will think I haven't done any work at all this morning."

She gazed gloomily into her basket. There were lots of lovely,

plump dewdrops left, but if she hung them up, would they just disappear, too?

Then Chloe had a brilliant idea. "Cockleshells and conkers!" she cried with a grin. "I know what I will do."

Carefully, she lifted out a shimmering dewdrop from her basket. She placed it gently on a silky strand of the nearest cobweb. Then Chloe added two more

43

dewdrops so that all three hung in a row, sparkling like precious jewels.

"Ah, well," Chloe declared loudly. "I think it's time that I went and had some breakfast." She gave her tummy a pat. "Ooh, I'm so hungry."

Chloe unfurled her wings and started to fly away. But instead of leaving Hawthorn Hedgerows, she swerved around the back of a large oak tree. Behind its huge trunk, Chloe was well hidden, but if she peeked out, she had a perfect view of the cobweb she had just decorated.

"Now all I have to do is wait," she said to herself, "and see if the dewdrop thief comes back."

45

Chloe waited. And as she waited, she began to wonder if her idea had been such a good one after all.

What if the dewdrop thief is very big? she thought.

The branches of the old oak tree creaked.

What if the dewdrop thief is scary?

A breeze shivered through the leaves.

What if the dewdrop thief doesn't like Cobweb Kittens?

There was a rustling in the hedgerow. Chloe peered around the tree. The thread of the silvery web was trembling and the dewdrops were quivering. Was the thief coming?

Chloe crouched down in her hiding place, not daring to look. The rustling stopped, and there was silence.

Gathering up all her courage, Chloe peeked out. What she saw wasn't big. And it wasn't scary. There, in the middle of the clearing, was a tiny Moss Mouse.

Moss Mice were another type of fairy animal. Their special job was to shape Misty Wood's moss

into velvety cushions for the other
animals to sleep on. But this timid
creature looked much too small
for any kind of job. He was just a
baby!

For a moment, the mouse sat all alone in the middle of the clearing. Then he tiptoed over to the hedge. With a flutter of his tiny wings, he flew up to the cobweb and began lapping thirstily at the nearest dewdrop.

Chloe stared in disbelief. To think that she had been scared of a terrible thief when all this time her hard work was being slurped up by a greedy mouse!

"What are you doing?" she cried, flying out from her hiding place.

The little Moss Mouse was so startled he fell backward from the web, did a somersault, and landed with a *plop* on a toadstool below. The dewdrops splashed down on top of him like rain.

"Those dewdrops are not for drinking. They're to make the hedges look pretty," Chloe

51

went on. "I spent ages hanging them."

But as she hovered above the Moss Mouse, Chloe saw that the water running down his pointy nose wasn't from the dewdrops. Big, splashy tears were spilling from his eyes and soaking his downy cheeks.

"I'm sorry," the little mouse said in a trembly voice. "But I was very thirsty, and I didn't know where

else to get a drink." He put his head
in his tiny paws and sobbed some
more.

Chloe felt awful. He was such
a young mouse, and he looked so
sad. She shouldn't have been cross
with him.

"It's all right," Chloe purred,
patting his back with her paw. "I'm
sorry I shouted at you. What's
your name, and why are you so
thirsty?"

"My name is Morris," the mouse sniffed. "I'm thirsty because I . . . I . . ." He started to cry again. "I lost my mommy and daddy."

"You *lost* them?" Chloe asked.

Morris nodded sadly.

"How did you lose them?"

Morris looked down. "We were going to visit Grandma," he whispered, "and I flew off to look at some buttercups. And then . . . and then . . . well, I couldn't find

54

my way back." He let out another tiny sob.

Chloe picked a velvety leaf from the hedge next to them and handed it to him. "Here," she said. "Wipe your eyes."

Morris dabbed at his face with the leaf.

"When did you lose your mommy and daddy?" Chloe asked.

"Yesterday morning," Morris replied.

55

"Yesterday morning?" Chloe stared at him. "No wonder you're thirsty."

"I was only going to drink one dewdrop," Morris whimpered, "but they were so tasty. I'm sorry." He hung his tiny head again.

Chloe thought of how the Stardust Squirrel had helped her when she'd lost her basket. Now it was her turn to help.

"Don't worry," she said with

57

a smile. "I'll help you find your mommy and daddy—I promise. Do you have any idea where your home is?"

Morris nodded. "It's by the lions."

Chloe stared at him in shock. "By the *lions*?"

"Yes," the little mouse replied. "By the big lions."

Chloe gulped. She didn't know there were lions in Misty Wood.

Her heart began to pound. Finding Morris's home might be a lot scarier than she had thought!

CHAPTER FOUR

The Rainbow Slide

Morris looked up at Chloe. His shiny black eyes blinked at her anxiously.

"Please will you take me home?"

he squeaked. "I miss my mommy and daddy."

Chloe's tummy gave a little lurch. She had to keep her promise. It was up to her to get Morris back safely, however scary it might be.

"Ladybugs and lollipops!" she whispered to herself. "If this little mouse is brave enough to live next door to some big lions, then as sure as my wings are purple, I am brave enough to take him there."

She turned to Morris again. "Is your home very far away?"

"Oh yes. Miles and miles," Morris replied.

"In that case," Chloe said, "I think it would be better if I carried you. Your wings are so small, and you must be very tired. You can climb onto my back. We'll fly above Misty Wood together. You can help me look out for the lions."

Morris clapped his tiny paws.

"Thank you! Thank you!" he squeaked excitedly.

Chloe tucked her basket of dewdrops beneath a hedge to keep it safe. Then she crouched down low as Morris clambered onto her back and perched between her wings.

"Hold on tight!" Chloe called. With a flick of her shimmering wings she flew up into the sky, brushing the treetops with her sparkly tail as she rose higher and higher.

"Wheeeeeeeee!" Morris cried.

Far below, Misty Wood lay
stretched out like a colorful
patchwork quilt, glimmering
in the early morning sunshine.
Somewhere down there, among
the meadows and the mountains,
the grasslands and the glades,
Morris's family was waiting
anxiously for him. But where were
they?

A flash of golden fur across

a patch of brilliant blue caught Chloe's eye.

Lions? Chloe caught her breath and looked closer.

No, it was only the Pollen Puppies. They were awake and playing in Bluebell Glade, flicking the pollen here and there with their tails so that even more flowers would grow.

I wonder if they know where the lions live, Chloe thought. She

called over her shoulder to her tiny passenger. "Hold on, Morris! We're going down!"

With a flutter of fairy wings, Chloe landed in the glade.

"Hey! What's going on?" Petey, a floppy-eared puppy, cried as he bounced over.

"Have you come to play with us?" his friend Max asked as he scampered up. Clouds of yellow pollen fell like gold dust from

his coat. "Look, everyone! It's a Cobweb Kitten who wants to be a Pollen Puppy."

"No, I don't wa—" Chloe began, but Max was already running around her, his tail wagging.

"First of all, you have to learn how to bark," Max said. "Show her how to bark, Petey."

"But I don't—" Chloe spluttered. Before she could say any more, Petey started barking.

"And wag your tail," Max called. "You have to wag your tail if you want to be a Pollen Puppy. It's what we do best."

Petey barked even louder, and other puppies started joining in,

too, until the whole glade became a
blur of wagging tails and barking
puppies.

"But—" said Chloe.

"Oh dear," squeaked Morris.

"*I don't want to bark and I don't want to wag my tail and I don't want to be a Pollen Puppy!*" Chloe shouted at the top of her voice.

The glade fell silent.

"Oh," said Petey.

"No need to shout," sniffed Max.

"I'm sorry," said Chloe. "I'm sure it's great fun being a Pollen Puppy, but something very sad has happened, and I need your help."

"Well, why didn't you say so?"
said Max.

"What's happened?" asked
Petey.

"When I was hanging up my
dewdrops this morning, I found this
little mouse." Chloe gestured with
her paw.

The puppies, who hadn't
noticed Morris because he was so
small, gathered closer.

"His name is Morris and he got

lost on the way to his grandma's, so I'm helping him find his way back home. But"—Chloe gulped and dropped her voice to a whisper— "Morris says he lives near some lions! Do you know if there are any lions living here in Misty Wood?"

"Lions?" A spotted puppy called Freckles started to laugh. "Has anyone seen any lions?"

"Grrr!" Max bared his tiny white teeth.

74

"Growl!" Petey sharpened his pointy claws.

"Roar!" Freckles shook his head so the pollen floated around his ears like a golden mane. "Lions, you say? Here we are!"

Chloe shook her head crossly. Usually the cheeky Pollen Puppies made her laugh, but this was no time for joking. She had to get Morris home.

"Please can you help me?" she begged. "Morris has been lost for a very long time."

At the sound of Chloe's sad voice, the puppies stopped their teasing.

"Sorry," said Max. "We were only joking."

"We really don't know where the lions live," Petey piped up.

"Hmm," said Freckles. "Why don't you try looking in Crystal Cave at the side of Heather Hill?"

"Crystal Cave? That's a great idea!" Chloe cried.

"You know how to get there, don't you?" said Max. "Just follow the rainbow."

"Thank you, puppies," Chloe said with a smile. "Hold on tight,

Morris. We're going up again!"

"Good-bye! Good luck!" the
Pollen Puppies called, their furry
tails waving wildly.

"And if you do ever want to be
a Pollen Puppy, just let us know,"
Max called out.

Crystal Cave was tucked away on
the very darkest side of Heather Hill.
Chloe knew exactly where to go.

Usually the sight of her favorite

78

hill, covered with pretty purple flowers, made her feel happy. Today, however, she felt scared. She had never seen a lion before, but she knew they were the biggest members of the cat family. *And a Cobweb Kitten is the smallest*, she thought nervously.

Now someone even smaller needed her help. Morris was counting on her to find his parents. She couldn't let him down.

79

Suddenly, there was a tiny shout in her left ear. "Look, Chloe!" Morris cried. "A rainbow! A rainbow!"

Sure enough, a rainbow of sparkling light arched across the sky in front of them. Chloe flapped her glittery wings with all her might until she landed on the very top of the rainbow.

"Hold tight, Morris! We're going for a ride!" she called over her shoulder.

"Wheeeeeeeee!" Morris squealed as they started to slide down the rainbow.

Faster and faster they slid. Chloe's whiskers tingled as the air whistled through them. Finally, they landed with a soft bump on the far side of Heather Hill, right at the mouth of Crystal Cave.

The warm colors of the crystals in the cave shimmered across Chloe's fur like fairy lights. For a

81

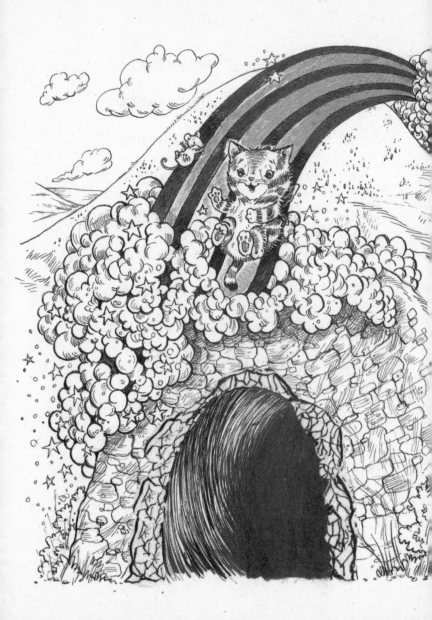

moment, she almost forgot what she was looking for. The rainbow ride had been so much fun and Crystal Cave was so pretty—it couldn't possibly be home to anything scary. Could it?

Suddenly, a very deep voice boomed out from the depths of the cave. "Who's there?"

Chloe fell back in fright.

"What do you want?" the voice rang out again.

Chloe crouched down. She was terrified.

On her back, Morris gave a small squeal and cowered into her trembling fur.

A dark shadow loomed out of the cave. Chloe could hardly bear to look. Were the Pollen Puppies right? Could this be the hiding place of a large and scary lion?

CHAPTER FIVE

Crystal Cave

"Well?" the voice boomed again. "I said, who's there?"

Chloe blinked against the dazzling light. "Oh!" she cried. "You're—"

"I'm what?" the figure boomed.

"You're not a lion!"

"Of course I'm not a lion!"

Chloe laughed with relief as the figure emerged. Now that he was standing in the sunlight, she could see he wasn't anything like a lion. He was a Bark Badger. From his broad black-and-white shoulders sprouted a pair of delicate, graying wings. The stocky creature shuffled forward and frowned down at them.

"Well," he said, "what do you little 'uns want? Apart from telling me that I'm not a lion!"

Chloe opened her mouth, but no sound came out. She might not have been face-to-face with a lion, but she *was* still a little scared.

Bark Badgers were very kind fairy animals, but they were also very big and strong. Their nimble paws carved the most beautiful patterns into the tree barks of Misty

Wood, and they took their job very seriously indeed. Unlike the cheeky Pollen Puppies, they had no time for jokes or tricks.

Gathering all her courage, Chloe raised her head and began to speak. "I'm helping this little Moss Mouse," she said with a trembling voice. "He's lost and I'm trying to find his home. He says it's near the lions, but I have no idea where the lions live. The

Pollen Puppies suggested I try looking here."

"Hmm." The Bark Badger stroked his whiskery chin thoughtfully. "Lions, you say?"

Chloe nodded.

"I have lived in Misty Wood forever and a day, and I have never known there to be lions here," the Bark Badger said.

"Oh, bother and broomsticks," Chloe said with a sad little sigh. "Will I ever get Morris home?"

The Bark Badger's wise black eyes began to twinkle. "I can see you are a very helpful and caring kitten," he said. "So I will give you

90

some advice. Are you listening carefully?"

Chloe leaned forward. "Oh yes," she said eagerly.

"There is a place in Misty Wood that is very dark and very quiet," the Bark Badger whispered in her ear. "No birds sing. No squirrels scamper. Everything is silent and still. It is in the Heart of Misty Wood, and few have ever been there." He tapped the side of his

nose knowingly with a long, pointy claw. "If there are lions in Misty Wood, that is where they will be hiding."

Chloe gave a small meow of fear. "Really, truly?" she whispered.

"Really, truly." The Bark Badger nodded.

"Oh. Well. Thank you," Chloe squeaked, trying to look braver than she felt. Her mind was racing. She had never ventured into the

Heart of Misty Wood before. It sounded very dark. And very scary.

"What did he say? What did he say?" Morris squeaked from her back.

"He said we are close to finding your home," Chloe replied. She couldn't let Morris know how nervous she was.

"Yippee! Yippee!" Morris cried, and did a little somersault behind Chloe's ear.

"Well, we'd better be off, then." Chloe smiled bravely at the Bark Badger. "Here I go. Into the Heart of Misty Wood." She paused. "Into the darkness," she went on, her voice wobbling ever so slightly.

"Perhaps you would like something to light your way?" the Bark Badger suggested.

Chloe smiled. "Oh yes, please."

The Bark Badger shuffled back into his cave and soon returned

94

with a piece of crystal taken from
the roof of the cave. It glowed with
so many different colors it was as if
he were holding a piece of rainbow.

"Thank you. It's very beautiful," Chloe breathed.

"You're welcome," the badger replied. "Now, hold it carefully ahead of you and let the light show you the way. Good-bye." The Bark Badger waved a large paw at them. "And good luck!"

Chloe flew up into the air, clutching the crystal tightly in her front paws. "Good-bye, Mr. Bark

96

Badger!" she called. "And thank you again!"

Soon they had left the beauty of Crystal Cave far behind and were venturing deeper into Misty Wood. Chloe held the rainbow crystal before her. Its warm glow lit up the gloom but also cast shadows that darted among the tree trunks. Sometimes it looked as if strange shapes were following them as they flew.

"It's so dark," Morris squeaked. "And scary, too."

"It's only the light playing tricks on us," Chloe said, trying to sound cheerful. "Now, Morris, do you recognize anything?"

"No," Morris replied sadly.

Chloe flew even deeper into the tangle of trees. It was very dark. And very quiet.

Up ahead, she saw two pinpoints of light coming from

the trunk of a tree. Then they disappeared. Then they beamed brightly at her once more. On and off, on and off the lights blinked.

Chloe's tummy gave a fearful lurch as she realized what she was looking at. They weren't lights.

They were eyes blinking at her from the dark.

CHAPTER SIX

A Magical Wish

Chloe meowed in surprise and
fluttered onto the solid branch of an
oak tree with a tiny thud.

"Ouch," Morris squeaked.

"Sshhhh," Chloe whispered, hardly daring to breathe. Up above her, the eyes blinked again. Chloe gulped. Had she found the lions at last?

The leaves on the tree above her started to rustle, and from the darkness came a soft noise. It sounded a bit like a lion, stretching its paws and shaking out its mane.

Chloe shrank back in fear as the leaves slowly parted to reveal

the eyes again, growing bigger and bigger.

But, to Chloe's relief, there was no lion's mane to be seen. Instead, the eyes were framed by the feathery face of an owl. A scarlet beak chirped a welcome.

"T'wit, t'woo! Who are *you*?"

Chloe gave a little sigh of delight. "Magic and milk shakes," she whispered softly to herself.

103

"Are you . . . are you . . . the Wise

Wishing Owl?"

The owl nodded three times.

Morris squeaked and Chloe

trembled with excitement. Never
in her wildest dreams had she
imagined she would come nose-to-
beak with the most magical animal
in all of Misty Wood.

The Wise Wishing Owl, with
her scarlet beak and feathers of
gold, was the cleverest and oldest
creature in the wood—as old as the
oldest oak trees. She had the power
to make wishes come true . . . if you
were able to find her.

"You are very far from home, little Cobweb Kitten. Are you lost?" The Wise Wishing Owl's voice was like the most beautiful piece of music Chloe had ever heard.

"Yes," Chloe said. "I'm trying to help this little Moss Mouse, Morris, find his family. I've been searching and searching, but I can't find them anywhere!" A silvery tear ran down Chloe's cheek, and she sniffed sadly.

"There, there, little kitten. Don't cry," the Wise Wishing Owl said. "You found me, and not many do. Now, do you have any idea where Morris might live?"

"Yes. He says he lives by the lions," Chloe answered with a gulp.

"The lions! The lions!" Morris squeaked.

"Oh." The Wise Wishing Owl furrowed her feathery brow. "I have lived in Misty Wood for a very,

very long time, but I have never heard of any lions living here."

Chloe gave a long, sad sigh. "That's what everyone says."

The Wise Wishing Owl turned her head slowly from side to side three times. "It helps me to think," she explained when she saw Chloe staring at her. "And now that I have thought, I believe I know where Morris lives."

"Hurray!" Morris squeaked.

"You do?" Chloe's face lit up with excitement. "Is it very far?"

"It certainly is," the Wise Wishing Owl said with a nod. "Perhaps I could have a word with young Morris?"

Chloe tilted her head.

"Hello, Morris," said the Wise Wishing Owl.

"Hello," Morris squeaked. "I've lost my mommy and daddy."

"I understand," said the Wise

Wishing Owl gently. "Now, let me ask you something. What is your dearest wish?"

"To find my mommy and daddy," Morris said with a little sigh.

"Then I shall grant your wish," the Wise Wishing Owl said solemnly.

"Hurray!" Morris cheered.

"Really?" Chloe asked.

"Of course," the Wise Wishing Owl replied. "I always help a fairy animal in need. You have done your best, Chloe, and I can see

you are very brave. But you also look very tired. Why not leave the rest to me?"

"Oh yes, please," Chloe said.

"Then hold on to your whiskers!" the Wise Wishing Owl hooted. "I'm sending you home." The owl flapped her huge wings up and down three times.

A gentle breeze began to play around the tree branch. Chloe felt a twig brush her face, and the breeze

grew stronger. Suddenly, she and Morris were lifted skyward. Up and up they spiraled, traveling faster with each twist and turn. Misty Wood spun beneath them, a blur of colors and light.

Chloe laughed excitedly. It was even better than sliding down the rainbow!

All of a sudden the spinning stopped, and they landed with a bump on the ground, a cloud of

114

yellow cushioning their fall.

"Lions!" Chloe gasped, her head still dizzy. But as her eyes adjusted to the bright daylight, she saw they hadn't landed on the back of a fierce yellow lion, but in a field of golden dandelions.

"Lions! Lions!" Morris cried in delight.

"Sunshine and sparkles!" Chloe said with a smile. "Look! We're in Dandelion Dell!" She stretched

115

out on the blanket of bobbing yellow flowers. "So you live by the *dande*lions, Morris."

"Yes! Yes!" Morris scampered down from her back and did a cartwheel in delight.

Chloe chuckled. "I should have known there wouldn't be any actual lions in Misty Wood."

Just then, there was a rustling sound in the dell. The dandelions started to sway. Something—or

116

someone—was making its way
toward them. Chloe heard a small,
high-pitched noise grow louder as it
got nearer.

"Morris, Morris, Morris,
MORRIS!"

Across the yellow field, a
procession of Moss Mice
appeared, marching through the
dandelions.

"Mommy! Daddy!" Morris
cried, and scampered into the arms

of two very relieved-looking Moss Mice. The rest of the procession cheered and waved.

Morris turned to Chloe. "My mommy and daddy! We found them!"

CHAPTER SEVEN

Home at Last!

As the Moss Mice gathered around, Chloe told them all about her and Morris's adventures.

"You thought we lived by some

scary lions?" Morris's mommy said, her eyes wide.

Chloe nodded.

"And yet you still tried to find us?" Morris's daddy asked.

Chloe nodded again.

"Well then, you are a very brave Cobweb Kitten," he said, and all the other Moss Mice started clapping and cheering in agreement.

Morris wriggled out of his

mommy's arms and scampered back up onto Chloe's back. "Thank you for helping me, Chloe," he whispered in her ear. "I'll never forget you."

Chloe fizzed with happiness to the very tips of her whiskers.

Morris's daddy clapped his paws. "Tell us, Chloe, is there any way we can repay you? We Moss Mice may be small, but we are very hard workers. If there is

122

anything you need, just let us know."

"Anything at all," Morris's mommy added.

Chloe scratched her head. "Thank you, but I can't think of anything I need, now that Morris is safe. I suppose I'd better get back to—" Chloe gasped. "Decorations and dandelions! My cobwebs!"

She looked at the sun, now high in the sky. It seemed very long ago

123

that she had woken with the sunrise

and set off to get her dewdrops.

"Yes, yes, there is something you

can help me with," she said eagerly.

Chloe had never flown with so many other fairy animals before. The Moss Mice spun and tumbled through the sky like dandelion seeds scattering on the breeze.

"Here we are!" Chloe cried at last, spotting the Hawthorn Hedgerows far below them.

In a swirl of excitement, the Moss Mice floated down to land in the clearing.

Chloe's basket of dewdrops was still where she had left it, tucked under one of the hedges. After

Chloe showed them what to do,
the Moss Mice set to work,
singing happy songs as they
scampered about. Soon, all
the cobwebs were decorated
with sparkling dewdrops, and
Hawthorn Hedgerows had never
looked so beautiful.

Chloe clapped with glee.

"Thank you!" she cried.

"Don't mention it," said Morris's daddy. "Now, after so much excitement, I think we all deserve a treat."

"Treat! Treat!" Morris cried.

"We shall have a picnic," Morris's daddy declared, and all the other mice started to cheer. "And, Chloe, you must be our very special guest."

Chloe was so happy she thought

she might burst. What a magical day it had been! She might not have found any lions, but she had certainly found plenty of new friends.

It was lovely living in Misty Wood.

☆ Misty Wood Quiz ☆

Misty Wood is home to all sorts of fairy animals. Which Fairy Animal would you be if you lived there? Take this fun quiz to find out.

 Misty Wood is full of beautiful things. Which of these do you think is the prettiest?

A) sparkly dewdrops
B) velvety green moss
C) a brightly colored flower
D) a floaty cloud of pollen

 Each fairy animal is cute and special in its own way. If you were a fairy animal, which of these would you most like to have?

A) silky fur
B) silver whiskers
C) soft, floppy ears
D) a fluffy, waggy tail

3 Of all the lovely places in Misty Wood, which is your favorite?

A) Dewdrop Spring
B) Dandelion Dell
C) Bluebell Glade
D) Honeydew Meadow

 4 The fairy animals stay cozy and warm at night. If you were a fairy animal, where would you like to sleep?

A) on a cozy cot of moss and soft grass
B) in a snuggly bed under an oak tree
C) in a lovely warm warren beneath a cluster of mulberry bushes
D) in a sweet little den under a hawthorn hedge

 5 Each fairy animal has a favorite thing to do in Misty Wood. What do you like doing the most?

A) decorating things and making everything around you look pretty
B) using your imagination to make things
C) playing with beautiful flowers
D) running, jumping, telling jokes, and playing games

Mostly A

You would be a Cobweb Kitten! Cobweb Kittens love pretty things, especially the glittery dewdrops they use to decorate the Misty Wood cobwebs. They enjoy collecting things in their baskets and drinking milk.

Mostly B

You would be a Moss Mouse! Moss Mice can be quite shy and quiet. They love stories and cuddling on their soft green cushions.

Mostly C

You would be a Bud Bunny! Bud Bunnies have cute, floppy ears and soft pink noses. They love playing in the sunshine with their friends, especially among the flowers.

Mostly D

You would be a Pollen Puppy! Pollen Puppies have loads of energy and like to run. They also love having fun and making other fairy animals laugh.

Misty Wood Treasure Hunt

Misty Wood is full of treasures, from the moonbeams in Moonshine Pond to a cave made of crystal and a rainbow to slide down. Try to find these treasures in your park or garden:

- A lovely green leaf
- A bright yellow dandelion
- A pretty feather
- A piece of velvety moss
- A prickly pinecone
- A snow-white daisy

Misty Wood Wishes

"T'wit, t'woo! I am the Wise Wishing Owl. I live in the Heart of Misty Wood. Not many people find me, but those who do may ask me to grant them their wishes."

If you could have three wishes granted by the Wise Wishing Owl, what would they be? You can write them below.

A wish for my best friend:

_____

_____

A wish for my mom or dad:

_____

_____

A wish just for me:

_____

_____

# of Misty Wood

Meet more Fairy Animal friends!